EXTINCTION LOST

USA TODAY BESTSELLING AUTHOR

NICHOLAS SANSBURY SMITH

OTHER BOOKS BY NICHOLAS SANSBURY SMITH

The Extinction Cycle Series (Offered by Orbit)

Extinction Horizon

Extinction Edge

Extinction Age

Extinction Evolution

Extinction End

Extinction Aftermath

Extinction Lost (A Team Ghost Short Story)

Extinction War (Coming Fall 2017)

Trackers: A Post-Apocalyptic EMP Series

Trackers 1

Trackers 2: The Hunted

Trackers 3: The Storm (Coming Winter 2017)

The Hell Divers Trilogy (Offered by Blackstone Publishing)

Hell Divers 1

Hell Divers 2: Ghosts (Coming July 18th, 2017)

Hell Divers 3: Deliverance (Coming 2018)

The Orbs Series (Offered by Simon451/Simon and Schuster)

Solar Storms (An Orbs Prequel)

White Sands (An Orbs Prequel)

Red Sands (An Orbs Prequel)

Orbs

Orbs II: Stranded

Orbs III: Redemption

Dear Extinction Cycle Reader:

Extinction Lost is a short story that first appeared in the Cohesion Press anthology SNAFU: Black Ops in December of 2016. If you have already purchased the Black Ops anthology you can return this short story for a refund through the vendor you purchased it through or by contacting me. If you haven't purchased it already, then you're in for a surprise. Extinction Lost may be short, but I think readers will enjoy this new Team Ghost mission, especially those of you waiting for Extinction Cycle book 7, War.

Speaking of Extinction War, I sincerely appreciate your patience while waiting for the next installment. Over the past three years I've worked tirelessly to publish the Extinction Cycle books in rapid fire to satisfy the demand. Over this time, the popularity of the series led to interest from both Hollywood and traditional publishers. In late 2016 I was approached with a publishing deal from Orbit, the science fiction imprint of Hachette. They are the publisher behind *The Remaining* series by DJ Molles and *The Expanse* by James S.A. Corey.

I'm excited to announce that Orbit will be re-releasing Extinction Cycle books 1-6 with new covers and in mass-market paperback! They will also publish book 7, *Extinction War* in November 2017. This means more readers will be able to experience the Extinction Cycle in a market where it wasn't available before—bookstores. Thank you to all of the fans that supported and continue to support Team Ghost and the Extinction Cycle story. Hopefully a movie or television series isn't too far off on the horizon...

If you have any questions, feel free to contact me at *greatwaveink@gmail.com*, or join my spam free mailing list to get notifications about Extinction War and my other books. Sign-up at: *http://eepurl.com/bggNg9*

"There are no shortcuts in evolution."
-Louis D. Brandeis

1

A DENSE SNOW FELL ON THE TEAM CROSSING THE tarmac toward the Sikorsky UH-60 Black Hawk chopper. Crew Chief Hector Webb zipped his parka up to his chin in an effort to keep out the chill. He hated the cold, especially in a place that kept getting colder. But unless the European Unified Forces—EUF—decided to nuke Greenland it was only going to get worse. Thankfully the trip to the island was a short one. The mission that had rerouted the USS *Forest Sherman* from the main European front would only take a couple of days.

Rubbing his gloved hands together, Webb watched Team Ghost moving as one across the deck of the destroyer. It was 0900 hours, but the sun was hiding in the blurry sky. The wind had picked up, sending walls of snow gusting across their path and covering their white fatigues in a blanket of white. The irony was striking, for a moment Team Ghost appeared as apparitions moving through the storm.

The leader, Master Sergeant Joe Fitzpatrick led the group with his German Shepherd trotting along at his side. Webb had heard the stories about the man and his dog single handily fighting thousands of Variants in New York City before Operation Extinction. There were countless tales of the two taking on formidable odds, but Webb's favorite was the one where Fitz had killed the Bone Collector Alpha with his bare hands. Apollo was said to have eaten the monster's heart.

Webb had his doubts, but if he was ever going to have a chance to ask, it would be on this flight. Perhaps he would even throw in a question about the legendary Captain Reed Beckham sending the dog to Europe with Fitzpatrick.

"Welcome aboard, Master Sergeant," Webb said.

Fitz nodded and climbed into the troop hold with his M4 and MK11. The gum-chewing female member of Team Ghost blew a bubble as she jumped inside. Rico tucked a frosted strand of pink hair under her stocking cap and helmet. Sergeant Hugh Stevenson climbed in next, a skull bandana around his throat—he cradled his M249 SAW. Staff Sergeant Blake Tanaka was the next one in. Webb checked the Katana long blade and the companion Wakizashi short blade strapped to Tanaka's back.

Damn, they are real.

He'd heard Tanaka had killed over a hundred Variants with them.

The others all carried silenced M4s, including Specialist Yas Dohi, who spat a licorice root out into the snow then pulled himself inside.

None of them said a word as they sat. Team Ghost was a diverse crew that was for sure; from their weapons to their nationalities.

Webb closed the door to seal out the cold then strapped in. He still couldn't believe he was about to embark on a mission with Team Ghost. Just seeing them here gave him chills. Tanaka, the short Japanese-American soldier with tree trunk legs and a shaved head twisted to adjust the strap of his blades. Dohi reached for another piece of licorice from his vest, and Rico pulled out a journal.

"You ready to rock it, Ghost?" asked the pilot, Ted 'Tito' Bones. He turned from the cockpit, scratching at his chin-strap beard with a grin.

Fitz gave a sluggish thumbs up and winced. That's when Webb noticed the bloodstain on the man's left shoulder. He wasn't the only injured one. Dohi, the Navajo tracker with jet-black hair and a silver goatee had a special chest brace.

Webb studied the other members of Ghost. Stevenson, the muscular African American man dipped his freshly-shaved face and closed his eyes. Rico wrote in her journal quietly. Tanaka put his ear buds in and drew in a breath. Dohi began tracing a finger around the bone handle of his knife.

They all looked exhausted.

"How long you been back from France?" Webb asked.

Fitz swiped a strand of red hair under his helmet. "Twenty hours."

Webb nodded because he didn't know what else to say. He had heard they'd hardly made it back from a mission to gather intel in France—intel that was vital to the next stage of the war—Operation Reach. Now Colonel Bradley was sending Ghost on another mission into enemy territory.

Several heads turned to the windows. Outside, a team of Marines boarded an adjacent Black Hawk. Another squad climbed into a third chopper. They were heading to Greenland with Team Ghost, but Webb wasn't sure exactly where the target was. His job was simply to man the door gun and assist with the flight, and he was glad for that, not just because of the cold, but because of the rumors about what dwelled on the world's largest island.

"ETA to target is about two hours," Tito said. "Depending on the storm. Sit tight, Ghost."

The rotors fired and made their first pass above, and Webb held his questions for later. He glanced out the window as the bird pulled into the sky. It only took a few minutes for the USS *Forest Sherman* to vanish on the horizon.

"All right, listen up everyone," Fitz said.

Tanaka pulled out his earbuds and Rico closed her journal.

"There's a reason Colonel Bradley sent us six hundred miles west of the European front, and that reason is Greenland..." Fitz hesitated as the chopper hit a stream of turbulence. The bulkheads rattled and he waited for it to pass.

"Got us some mean looking skies," Tito said. "Better hold on to your breakfast."

The bird vibrated, jerked, and then steadied out. Webb eyed the fort of clouds they were headed for. The other two Black Hawks were about to enter the storm. One by one, the wall swallowed the choppers.

Fitz waited another second before continuing.

"Here's a timeline of events. VX9H9 was deployed over Greenland not long after the outbreak so about six or seven months ago. Kryptonite was deployed two months ago. The surviving government and military reached out to General Nixon about a week ago stating the weapons have worked well in most areas..."

"Except the one we are going to," Stevenson said, shaking his head.

"Correct..." Fitz pulled out a laminated map and held it up for his team to see. "But our mission isn't to determine why." He paused again and scratched at the stubble on his jaw like he didn't want to say what came next.

"Anyone ever heard of the German fortress Hitler was supposed to escape to in Antarctica?" he finally asked.

Rico chuckled. "Sure. The US supposedly launched Operation Highjump there. Story goes they sent ground and air forces to fight the Nazis at their base in the Queen Maud Land of Antarctica. The Germans were said to have UFOs and all sorts of—"

"That shit wasn't real, Rico," Stevenson interrupted.

Fitz directed his gaze at Rico and then Stevenson, silencing them quickly.

"Stevenson is right about Antarctica, but what I was getting to is that there *was* a Nazi base in Greenland not far from this Inuit fishing village," Fitz said. He pointed at the map and Rico sheepishly raised her hand.

Fitz dipped his chin at her.

"I thought the Nazis only had a weather station in Greenland."

"That's what everyone thought, until now."

Dohi pulled his knife and twirled it nimbly despite the rattle of turbulence. If anyone else was doing it, Webb might have told them to stop.

"Nazis? UFOs? What the hell are you guys talking about?" Stevenson asked. "I mean, seriously, what the fuck?"

Rico ignored him and directed her attention to the leader of Team Ghost. "Do you think that base has something to do with Kryptonite not working on the Variants there?"

Fitz folded the map in half, and then into a quarter to examine it closely. "That's what we're going to find out," he said. "The government retrofitted the base into a lab and were working on a bioweapon of their own to kill the juveniles."

"I don't suppose these 'rebels' are going to help us, either, are they?" Tanaka said. "Not that I'm complaining. Just saying. The EUF wasn't there for Operation Beachhead either."

Fitz gave a reply with a quick shake of his head.

"What about the locals?" Rico asked. "Are there any still alive? Perhaps they could give us some intel if there are any out there."

"Maybe if any of them are still alive," Fitz replied. He went back to studying the map as turbulence rattled the chopper. Webb used the time to check the sky. He still couldn't see the other Black Hawks.

"Our orders are to find and infiltrate the facility and destroy whatever weapon they were working on," Fitz continued. "When we're finished, we're ordered to destroy the old Nazi facility."

"And I don't suppose you know what this weapon does, do you?" Dohi asked.

Fitz pulled a small handheld recorder from his rucksack and held it up. "This tape is the only real intel I have. It came from a joint mission between the Greenland military and the EUF. Most of it's in English."

Every member of Team Ghost moved closer to Fitz, even Apollo, who sat on his haunches. Webb unclipped his harness so he could hear.

Fitz clicked the play button.

Background noise, hardly audible over the whoosh of the helicopter blades, broke from the tiny speakers. A voice cracked through a moment later.

"Command, we have found the tunnel to the facility, permission to enter."

"Copy that, Eagle 1, green light."

A few seconds of static passed, followed by a panicked voice. "We're entering the labs. Something happened here… something awful. There are bones and some sort of…"

More static, then the same frightened voice.

"There's something here, Command."

There was gunfire from multiple rifles.

"Lee is gone!" someone else said. "Shit they got Galan, too!"

Webb shuddered at the piercing hiss and shriek that followed.

"Eagle 1, do you copy?"

"Wolf 1, do you copy?"

"Snake 1, do you copy?"

"Command, Snake 1, we're cut off from the other teams… we have multiple contacts… What the hell is that thing!"

"Take it down, Bray!" someone shouted.

Another flurry of gunshots sounded. What came next made Webb swallow hard. The high-pitched shriek almost sounded human.

The tape cut off, and silence filled the troop hold.

Fitz lowered the recorder and scanned his team. Their faces were stone cold, but Webb could feel his own eyes widen from shock.

"That was the last anyone heard from the strike teams," Fitz said.

"How many were there?" Stevenson asked.

"Three teams. About thirty men. Not a single one made it out."

Stevenson made a low whistle.

"Damn," Tanaka added. "So that's it? They didn't send in any more teams to figure out what the hell is down there?"

"They don't have any to spare," Fitz replied.

Stevenson shook his head. "Of course not. Just like the EUF couldn't spare anyone to help the 24th MEU during Operation Beachhead. Why the fuck don't they just bomb the site?"

The chopper hit another pocket of turbulence. Webb grabbed a handhold and looked out the window at fluffy white clouds and snowflakes pelting the window. He searched for the other Black Hawks while Fitz continued his briefing.

"Nixon wants that weapon destroyed internally. We can't risk it getting out. Bombs could bury it, but..."

Webb focused on a flash of motion through the clouds to the east.

"Three American fire-teams against a Nazi base full of God knows what…" Stevenson started to say.

"I'll take those odds any day," Rico said.

Dohi agreed with a grunt. "Me too."

The underbelly of the bird seemed to answer with a groan as they passed through another stronghold of air.

"Jesus," Rico said. She grabbed her stomach. "This is one hell of a rough flight."

Webb glimpsed another flash of movement in the sea of white. He leaned in closer for a better view at a gap in the clouds. Every helmet in the troop hold looked in his direction at the sudden distant crack of gunfire.

"Ghost, we got Reavers!" Tito immediately said over the comms. "Badger 1 is under attack!"

Fitz hurried over to Webb. They opened the door and a blast of cold air swirled into the troop hold.

"You got eyes?" Fitz asked.

Webb shook his head, and then froze. Through the thinning clouds he saw something that seized the air from his chest.

A dozen massive bird-like Variants swooped around Badger 1. The Marine on the M240 blasted away at the monsters while his comrades open fired with their M4s. Badger 2 was to the east, flying adjacent, and holding their fire.

Webb tried to move, but the sight of the Reavers had him paralyzed with fear. He had never seen one in real life. Their armored bodies and fleshy wings flapped through the sky, surrounding Badger 1 like Turkey Vultures waiting to feed.

A round punched through the bulkhead behind Webb,

snapping him from his trance. He ducked with the rest of Team Ghost.

"Holy shit! They aren't watching their fire zones!" Rico shouted.

"Tito, get us clear!" Fitz ordered.

Webb turned for the M240, but Dohi was already manning the gun. He raked the muzzle back and forth for a clear shot.

One of the Variants plucked a Marine from the open doorway of Badger 1 and tossed him into the clouds. Three of the creatures dropped into a nosedive after the man while one of the smaller beasts flapped into the troop hold. It knocked three of the Marines out the other side like bowling pins.

Webb felt his heart rising in his throat as the remaining Marine fired at the Reaver that had climbed inside the craft. The beast retracted its wings so it could fit then slashed the man with a pair of talons, slicing him across the neck. He dropped his weapon and grabbed at the wound, stumbling backward.

Screaming filled the open channel as the pilots tried to keep the bird in the air. They pulled up hard and a body fell from the chopper, vanishing into the clouds. In a matter of minutes, the beasts had killed every Marine in the troop hold, leaving the pilots on their own.

The Reaver got on all fours and crawled up to the cockpit. It retracted a spiked tail, and then impaled one of the pilots like a scorpion hitting prey with its stinger. The other pilot turned from the cyclic stick and fired an M9.

A loud crack sounded to Webb's left. He cupped a hand

over his ears and watched the head of the Reaver explode inside the Black Hawk. Ears ringing, he turned to see the smoking barrel of Fitz's MK11 sniper rifle.

When Webb looked back to Badger 1, it was gone, hidden by the cloud cover. Dohi remained calm and steady on the big gun, scanning for a target.

Snow tore into the side of the troop hold, and the cold bit through Webb's layers. He let out a breath in a puff. The blades thumped above them, and for a moment it seemed like everything had slowed to a stop.

When the clouds finally cleared Webb searched for Badger 1, but where there should have been a Black Hawk, there was only open sky.

Stevenson broke the silence. "Odds just got worse, Rico."

Apollo let out a whine as Fitz lowered his rifle. "Keep your eyes peeled," he said. "Those things are still out there."

Webb tried to nod, but he just stood there shivering, and not from the cold. Team Ghost had already lost a fire team, and they weren't even at the target yet.

2

Master Sergeant Joe Fitzpatrick had planned on taking a nap on the helicopter ride, but instead he spent the trip watching the sky for Reavers with the rest of his team.

Badger 1 was gone… lost in an attack by monsters that should never have been out this far. Webb, the Crew Chief, had said they were migrating to find food. On top of the attack, Fitz had other worries on his troubled mind. Rumors had reached the European front that something was happening back in the States—rumors of a coup, and attacks on Safe Zone Territories.

Fitz winced as he twisted in his seat toward the cockpit. He had to keep frosty. Worrying about his friends back home wasn't going to do any good when he was all the way out here and couldn't do anything to help them.

"Tito, how far?" he asked.

"Five minutes from the target."

Jagged mountains rose along the coast in the distance. Below, icebergs floated through the blue water like ice cubes. A wall of mist covered a harbor full of fishing boats and drifted up toward the rocky shoreline.

Fitz strained for a better look for the small fishing village. Most of the residents were Inuit, but there were several locals living here that had worked for the government and in the top-secret lab.

Badger 2 pulled alongside and together, the two choppers flew inland. They passed over rocky beaches and turned toward a road that curved along the shore. On the top of a hill overlooking the harbor, the first houses finally came into view. Wood structures with peeling red and blue paint lined the elevated terrain like colorful gravestones.

Tito and his co-pilot circled along with Badger 2. The main city was just three blocks of aging structures. From above, Fitz couldn't see much. Snow covered the terrain and most of the road.

Dohi looked back from the door gun.

"No sign of tracks down there," he said. "Variant or human. But the snow could have hidden any recent activity."

Fitz nodded back. They were about to drop into a ghost town and he had no doubt the monsters were hiding somewhere down there. He just hoped they weren't going to run into anything like the abominations in France. Black Beetles, Pinchers, Wormers, or God only knew what else was out there. Part of him was glad to have a break from Europe.

He stood and looked for a spot to land. A red church

with a short steeple sat on a cliff overlooking the harbor. There was plenty of room for a landing zone there.

"Tito, take us down by that church."

"You got it."

Fitz reached down to check Apollo's vest. The dog had suffered another injury at the Basilica of St Thérèse in Lisieux, France, but hadn't required stitches like Fitz's shoulder.

Apollo licked Fitz's hand and rubbed his wet muzzle against his arm.

"Hold still, boy," Fitz said. He grabbed dog boots from his pack and then slipped them over the Shepherd's paws one at a time.

Apollo didn't like that. He swiped at the ground, trying to remove them, but instantly stopped when Fitz shook his head.

Glancing up with sad, amber eyes, the dog obeyed his handler.

Wind from the rotors whipped up the snow covering the LZ, forming a circular mound several feet deep. Tito and his co-pilot hovered over the church and waited for Fitz's orders.

"All right, Ghost. Lock and load."

Webb stepped up to the open door and glanced down.

"Look's clear, Tito," he said.

Tito slowly lowered the chopper as Team Ghost slapped magazines in their weapons and applied final layers of clothing. Fitz pulled the laughing joker bandana he'd inherited from Staff Sergeant Alex Riley, around his face. He closed his eyes and exhaled in an effort to keep the painful memories from muddling his thoughts.

All it takes is all you got, Marine.

He slung his MK11 over his back and pulled his suppressed M4. After palming in a magazine, Fitz stepped to the open door. Wind gusted below from the rotors, stirring up more of the white grit.

He eyed the landscape one more time for contacts. The church, terrain, and road beyond were clear.

"Take us down!" Fitz yelled over the noise.

Tito lowered them a few feet from the ground without touching down.

"Go, go, go!" Fitz yelled. He put a hand on Rico's back and patted her. She jumped out after Dohi and Stevenson. Fitz waited for Tanaka and then grabbed Apollo under the belly.

"Good luck, Master Sergeant!" Webb shouted. "I look forward to hearing of your victory!"

Fitz looked at the middle-aged crew chief. He had the timid stare of a man that had never seen combat. But that wasn't the only reason Fitz knew he had never fought a Variant. No one that had fought the monsters would look forward to hearing a story like that.

"Good luck, brother," Tito said over the comms.

Fitz nodded and jumped out. His blades sank into the powder and he ducked and ran toward the church. Badger 2 came in next, disgorging the six Marines of Fox Team. Like Ghost, the men were all dressed in white camouflage. They shouldered their M4s and swept the muzzles across the terrain.

Surrounded by his men, Sergeant Jackson Mapes jogged over to Fitz carrying a Benelli M4 tactical shotgun. He was one of the shortest Marines Fitz had ever met, but what

Mapes lacked in height, he made up for in muscle and speed. At forty-five, he was still one of the fastest Marines in the 24th MEU.

"Form a perimeter," Mapes said to his men. They fanned out, and took knees with their rifles pointed in all directions. The exposed faces Fitz could see all looked young, far too young to be out here. But that was partly due to a new rule. The military now allowed anyone over the age of sixteen to join.

"Dohi, you and Tanaka do some quick recon. Don't go out too far," Fitz said.

The men were running before Fitz had finished his sentence. He watched the choppers traverse the skyline as Stevenson and Rico took up position with the members of Team Fox.

Tito and the other pilots were headed to a small rebel-run outpost forty minutes away. Forty minutes was a hell of a long time if Ghost and Fox ran into trouble. But it beat having to wait if the choppers went all the way back to the USS *Forest Sherman*.

Fitz drew in a breath of icy air through his bandana.

"Master Sergeant, this sure as hell doesn't look like the foothills to me. I don't reckon you know where the hell we are, do ya?" Mapes asked. A thin layer of snow stuck to the man's graying five o'clock shadow. His breath reeked of cigarettes, and his crooked teeth reflected years of coffee drinking.

"We're approximately three miles from the target," Fitz said. "Figured it would be safer to hike in and clear the town of any hostiles first."

Mapes raised a bushy eyebrow. "A three mile hike in this weather could take us a while, especially if we have problems along the way."

"I'm not waltzing into the facility without knowing what we're up against. The evidence is in this village. If someone is still alive here then maybe we can figure out what happened," Fitz said firmly. He pulled his map out again and gestured for Rico and Mape to crowd around.

"You think someone could have survived in this shit hole of a village?" Mapes asked.

"We're going to find out," Fitz replied. "There are a dozen houses and other buildings between here and the target. I'm recommending we split up to search some of them."

Mapes picked at a gap between his yellow teeth, a nervous tick. It was his way of saying he didn't agree. Fitz noted it with a grain of salt.

"Sergeant, you take Fox this route." Fitz traced a line northwest through the village toward the foothills. "I'll take Ghost to search this route and we rally here, at the target."

"And if it's not there?" Mapes asked.

"Then we search until we find it."

"Weather is getting worse," Rico said.

The light snowfall had turned into flurries. Fitz squinted at the sheets of snow in the distance. He could hardly see the house at the top of the hill.

"We rally in two hours," Fitz said. "If you find anything, you radio it in, but otherwise, radio silence."

Mapes dipped his helmet, slightly. Another tell.

"You got it, Sergeant?" Fitz asked.

"Yes."

Fitz directed his gaze at Rico. "You and Stevenson clear the church before we head out."

"Master Sergeant."

The voice pulled Fitz to his left. Dohi was there, his eyes sharp and intense. His tan skin was red from the cold, but he had insisted on not wearing any facial protection. Fitz was afraid to ask what had the big man spooked.

"Tanaka and I found something..." Dohi said. "You better come take a look."

Flurries fell to the ground, adding a fresh layer of powder that crunched under Fitz's blades. He followed Dohi and Tanaka around the back of the church with Apollo trotting behind him. The rest of Ghost and Fox held the perimeter.

Fitz raised his rifle to scan the gray sky and the harbor over the cliffs. The slight movement prompted a jolt of pain across his raw injury. The stitches tightened every single time. It was a small price to pay. He had walked away from the battle at the Basilica St Thérèse with his life, something countless innocents couldn't say. Memories of Michel, the other children that had died there with their brave caretaker, Mira, were tattooed on his mind.

All it takes is all you got Marine.

He blinked away the memory and kept moving.

Ahead, Dohi pointed at a wood shed with double doors. The one on the right was frozen shut, but the left door was slightly ajar.

Using his fingers, Dohi told the story. No contacts, but

there was something inside. Fitz lowered his rifle as he walked the five steps to the open door. He took in a breath to test for the rotting, sour-fruit smell of the monsters. There was a trace of sweat and saliva on his bandana, but nothing to indicate Variants.

Dohi flipped on a light and directed it inside. "Take a look."

Fitz followed Dohi and Tanaka through the opening expecting to find a stack of frozen bodies like Team Ghost had discovered in Building 8 over seven months ago. But this was not a meat locker.

They had stepped into a single tomb.

"What the fuck?" cracked a voice.

Sergeant Mapes stood behind them, staring at the same narrow, seven-foot wood cross Dohi had discovered. Instead of a crucified model of Jesus hanging on the cross there was a juvenile Variant.

Or at least Fitz thought it was. Where there should have been armor plates covering its extremities there were ribbons of exposed muscle, stretched and purple from the cold. Icicles hung from the sucker-mouth on the beast's face. Ribs were cracked and flayed open like a grenade had exploded inside its chest. The organs, stomach, and intestines were all missing.

Fitz recalled the tape they had heard on the flight in.

There are bones and some sort of...

Had the military stumbled across something similar inside the lab?

"What the hell happened to this thing?" Tanaka said. He pulled his Katana and used the tip of the blade to raise the beast's chin for a better look.

"Jesus," Fitz whispered.

Empty sockets greeted them, only strings of muscle where the eyes had once been. Fitz couldn't pull his gaze from the anatomy. He had never seen the inside of a juvenile before. What little left there was to see…

Tanaka sheathed his sword and stepped back. "This is some truly evil shit. What do you make of it, Fitz?"

"I've never seen anything like it… I mean, I have, but not from juveniles. Variants do this to one another, and to humans, but I've never witnessed this behavior from the offspring."

Fitz studied Dohi for a reaction, but the man simply stroked the ice out of his silver goatee.

"We should get moving," Mapes said. "We're wasting time in here."

Fitz glanced at the monster one last time, his guts twisting. Something was very off in this fishing village, and he had a feeling it all had to do with the buried Nazi facility they were supposed to find and destroy.

They returned to the church where the other team members were waiting. Stevenson and Rico stood on the front steps, weapons cradled and relaxed.

"You find anything?" Fitz asked.

"Nothing alive," Stevenson said. "What about you?"

"Nothing alive," Fitz replied.

Stevenson smirked and Fitz walked up the steps to peer into the church. Snow swirled inside from the gust behind him, a mini tornado whipping the grit down a row of pews and up into the rafters. A Christian cross with a model of Jesus hung above an altar at the other end of the room.

The sight made Fitz shudder. He performed the sign of the cross and closed the doors to seal the room. The other soldiers continued raking their muzzles across the terrain around the church.

"All right Ghost and Fox, we're moving out," Fitz said. "Good luck, Sergeant."

Mapes simply nodded and waved Fox away from the church. His men fanned across the snowy terrain and moved northwest. Within moments the wall of flurries had swallowed them.

Fitz didn't like splitting up, especially after what they had discovered in the shed, but one thing he had learned over the past seven months was that you never put all your eggs in one basket. It had almost destroyed the American military during Operation Liberty. They were already down a fire team, and someone had to complete this mission.

"Combat intervals, Ghost," Fitz said. "Dohi, you got point. Stevenson, you're on rear guard. Rico and Tanaka you stay close to me and Apollo. High and low, watch the rooftops and sky for Reavers."

"I can't even see the sky," Stevenson said.

"Do your best," Rico said.

As Dohi raised his gun and walked past, Fitz reached out to stop him. "You all right, brother? I can put someone else on point."

"I'm fine, Master Sergeant," Dohi replied confidently. He spat a chunk of licorice root into the snow and jogged ahead. He was definitely moving slower than normal, and Fitz could tell the man's ribs and his head were bothering him, but Dohi was the last one to ever complain. When he did talk, it wasn't about himself.

Team Ghost set off to the northeast, following Dohi up a curving road that was hardly visible under the drifting white. There were still no signs of tracks. Even the tire marks were buried.

The whistling wind echoed as they began their hike. It rose and fell like waves slapping then receding at the beach. Fitz kept to the road where his blades sank through only several inches, crunching the gravel beneath.

Apollo trotted ahead, sniffing the snow every few feet. Team Ghost watched their zones of fire with muzzles sweeping for hostiles, moving with calculated precision. Fitz pushed his scope to his snow goggles to scan the sky again. If the Reavers were out there, he wouldn't have much warning. The road, framed on both sides by mounds of snow and red wood houses, provided little cover. They were sitting ducks out here for the winged abominations and whatever else prowled in the quaint fishing village.

A voice over the wind snapped him from his thoughts.

"What did you see back there, Fitzie?"

He lowered his scope to see Rico walking to his left. The frosted pink tips of her hair protruded from her stocking cap and helmet. Her dimples widened as she chewed on a stick of bubble gum.

"Juvenile corpse..." He didn't want to spook her, but she had a right to know. "Flung up on display like a macabre shrine."

Rico stopped dead in her tracks. "What... What do you mean?"

"Some sort of science experiment. Hell if I know. I don't know what it means, or who did it."

Rico gave him a meaningful look before she shouldered her rifle. "I don't like this, Fitzie. I don't like this one damn bit."

The howling wind seemed to answer her.

Fitz pushed on, his blades crushing the compact powder into the gravel. The cold was slowly working into his layers and his fingers were icing inside of his gloves. He moved them to keep the blood flowing. They had hiked for ten minutes, and he was already cold.

A sensation of being watched stopped him mid-stride.

"What is it?" Rico asked, slowly turning with her rifle.

"Something's out there… watching us from afar. Studying… scrutinizing us."

"You're freaking me out."

"Sorry. Just keep your eyes peeled." He slowly scanned the terrain and the sky. The creatures had evolved to see in the dark, but could they see through the dense sheets of snow?

Fitz continued toward the hilltop. According to the map, the village was on the other side. Dohi stopped near the top, crouched, and balled his hand into a fist. Then he got onto his stomach and scoped the village below. A wave of snow glided over his body as he lay there, still like a fox waiting out prey.

Fitz hung back with Rico and the others. He pulled his bandana down and wiped his fogged snow goggles while they waited. Dohi had the best eyes, ears, and nose in the team. He was a full-blooded Navajo tracker, and Fitz was glad to have him. If anyone could sense the monsters coming, it was Dohi and Apollo.

A flash of motion came from the hill as the drifting snow cleared. Dohi stood and gave the all clear to advance. He continued over the other side with Tanaka running to catch up. Blasts of wind tore into Fitz as he followed. He pulled his bandana back up, tucked his helmet down, and fought the current of air.

Better get used to Command sending Team Ghost into a shit storm. Just like in France, Ghost was getting the hard assignments—the missions no one else could complete. Fitz was starting to wonder if he was ever going to make it back to Plum Island to see his friends. As soon as this mission was over he was going to figure out exactly what the hell was going on back in the States. Someone had to know…

When he reached the crest of the hill he stopped to get his bearings. Apollo was just ahead, and Rico was still by his side. He used a sleeve to brush away the ice clinging to his eyebrows.

The road dipped into a valley protected from the wind. White rooftops dotted the landscape. He counted thirteen structures, all of them spread out along three main streets. Several vehicles caked in snow sat idly on the road. Dohi and Tanaka were already making their way toward a truck.

Fitz stood there for another second, staring at the snowy structures of a village that seemed frozen in time. From his vantage, it looked like the inside of a snow globe.

"You coming?" Rico asked.

Fitz nodded and ran down the slope toward the vehicles. By the time they caught up with Dohi and Tanaka they had already cleared the truck. Like the church, it was empty. He was starting to get the feeling they weren't going to find anyone alive here.

Stevenson pulled his skull bandana down and spat in the snow.

"Where the fuck are all the bodies?" he asked. "Even the Variants leave behind skeletons."

Apollo's tail was still up, which was the only good sign Fitz had seen yet. The dog didn't sense any monsters in the vicinity.

"Come on, we need to keep moving," Fitz said.

Team Ghost continued down the road that led to the central part of the village. The first block was comprised of businesses—a hardware shop, café, and a police station. The other signs were too covered in snow to make out. More houses lined the second and third blocks. Abandoned cars sat in the streets, doors frozen shut.

Fitz motioned for the team to spread out down the first block. There was no way they were going to clear each structure, but they had to figure out what the hell happened to these people. It might be the only way to understand what had happened inside the lab.

Fitz flashed signals, splitting the team up. Dohi and Tanaka took off across the street to clear the hardware store. He directed Stevenson to hold security in the street while Rico and Apollo followed Fitz toward a café.

He raised his silenced M4 toward a shattered front door. Shards of glass framed the wood, but a mound of snow had formed on the other side. He reached for the handle to pull it open, but it wouldn't budge.

Rico was already looking for an alternate route in. She walked along a still-intact rectangular window. Drawings of steaming coffee mugs and plates of fish marked the icy glass.

Fitz and Apollo followed her to the corner to a small alley that separated the building from the adjacent structure. Snow swirled into the narrow passage, masking his view momentarily. When it cleared he saw a back door to the café. From the sidewalk, he checked the rest of his team before entering.

Stevenson crouched on the sidewalk and nodded to Fitz.

Across the street, Dohi and Tanaka had already entered the hardware store.

With a breath, Fitz followed Rico into the alley. She stopped at the door, grabbed the handle, and put her shoulder into it after Fitz gave her the okay. Ice fell away from the frame and it creaked open.

Rico stepped back and shouldered her rifle.

Apollo stood next to Fitz, waiting for orders.

"Execute," Fitz said.

Rico kicked the door, and Fitz strode inside, sweeping his rifle back and forth over an empty kitchen.

Pots, pans, and glasses littered the floor.

Apollo sniffed the ground, wagged his tail, and sat on his haunches.

"Clear," Fitz said. He exchanged a glance with Rico. Side by side, they pointed their muzzles toward an open door that led to the main dining area. They slowly walked into the room furnished with booths and tables, clearing opposite sides.

Fitz lowered his rifle and let out an icy plume of breath

that quickly faded away. The surface of every table and chair was covered in a layer of snow.

"Not even a single body," Rico said.

She stepped over to a booth and wiped off the snow with her glove, revealing dinner plates and mugs. A bowl of frozen soup sat in the center of the table.

"It's like they got up and left in the middle of dinner," Fitz whispered. He scanned the room, then jerked his chin toward the exit.

They returned to the sidewalk just as Dohi and Tanaka exited the building across the street.

Both men shook their head.

Fitz mimicked their action and turned to wave Stevenson over, but the big man was gone.

Fitz whirled to his left, then his right.

"Stevenson?" Fitz said. "Yo, Stevenson." He kept his voice low, trying not to draw attention, but the only answer was the whistling wind.

Dohi and Tanaka crossed the street, battling gusts of snow and grit.

"Where the fuck did Stevenson go?" Rico asked.

Fitz ran to the position he had last seen the man. He slowed as he spotted a wad of black material resting in the fresh powder. Stevenson's crumpled skull mask bandana.

3

SERGEANT MAPES COULDN'T BELIEVE HIS LUCK. JUST when things were rolling forward with Operation Reach in Europe, he was sent to Greenland. Fucking Greenland. What the hell did the United States care about Greenland? He shook his head and continued the march through the western edge of a fishing village with a name he couldn't even pronounce.

The worst part wasn't getting shipped off to this oversized hunk of ice though. It was not knowing if he could trust the new members of his team. He had lost four on the landing in France. Four new faces, four new names, and four new Marines he had to babysit surrounded him in the flurries. The only Marine he trusted was Corporal Mark Carol.

Mapes tucked the butt of his M4 tactical shotgun in the

sweet spot in his armpit and continued walking. Carol was on point with his SAW slowly moving back and forth for contacts.

Lance Corporal Dixon and Lance Corporal Preston were working the road to the right. Both men were young, just seventeen and eighteen years old. A little younger than Mapes had been when he joined the Corps. It seemed like a hell of a long time ago in some ways, but in others he could still remember the first time he got an ass whooping for failing to polish his boots properly.

Oorah.

The good old days when they were fighting men, not monsters.

He looked to the other two members of his team, Lance Corporal Johns and Lance Corporal… Shit, Mapes had forgotten the name of the other man. His last name was a big city. He could remember that much.

Boston. You idiot.

Lance Corporal Boston and Lance Corporal Johns owned the road to the left. They were young bloods as well. Mapes hadn't had the chance to get to know any of the new men, and he was still grieving the loss of those that had come before them. But this was war, and he knew by the time it was over there would be more fresh faces on Fox Team. One of them might end up replacing his own.

He continued through the snowstorm toward a cluster of shacks. Lumpy, white foothills rose like toes on a frozen foot in the distance. The road curved through the small fishing community nestled at the edge. Lines hung from poles in the yards where the owners had thrown up fresh catches to dry out. This was where the locals had lived, in poverty, without any form of electricity from what Mapes could tell.

He sniffled and swallowed a hunk of mucus. It caught in his throat, and he hocked it up, and spat it into the snow. On top of everything, he was catching a damn cold. He hated the fucking cold, hated the cold more than anything. If he ever did make it out of this mess and had the luxury of retiring he was going to do it somewhere warm, like Florida, or perhaps Mexico.

Damn you, Master Sergeant Fitz.

Mapes didn't care how many Alphas and Variants Fitz had brought down. Trekking through the village was stupid and a waste of time. They should have dropped in outside the target and infiltrated the facility right away.

Carol balled his hand into a fist as he reached the first house. Then he directed his SAW at a single-room structure to his left.

Mapes jogged to catch up.

"What you got, Carol?"

He pointed toward a mound of white fur sticking out behind the right side of the house. It was the first sign of anything, alive or dead, that Mapes had seen since they began the trek thirty minutes ago.

He motioned for Dixon and Preston to clear the adjacent house. The men dipped their helmets and took off through the snow. Mapes left Johns and Boston to hold security on the side of the road, then jerked his chin for Carol to follow.

Together, the veteran Marines slowly approached what looked like a wolf pelt. Mapes had heard of the furry Variants discovered in climates just like this. The thought sent a shiver up his back. He had killed all sorts of monsters in the past seven months, but there was no denying an abominable snowman Variant with sucker lips was at the top of his list for the most horrifying things he could meet.

Jesus Christ. Is this real life?

Mapes knew Jesus wasn't going to save him from anything. He flicked the safety off his shotgun. The only thing that had his back was the 12-gauge he was holding.

The wind howled in the distance. A gust scraped a chunk of snow off the shack's roof, and it punched through the fresh powder. He eyed the foot-long icicles hanging from the awning as he hugged the wall. The last way he wanted to die in the apocalypse was from a spear of ice driven through his skull.

Mapes could already hear what they would say about him back on the European front lines.

You hear what happened to Mapes? The dummy got hit in the dome by a spear of ice.

He shook his head and focused on the white fur that was ruffling in the wind. With his left side close to the shack, he inched forward, Carol on his right flank.

They exchanged a nod, and Carol burst around the corner with his SAW at eye level. Mapes moved his finger from the trigger guard to the trigger. Static crackled in his ear as he directed his shotgun on a corpse partially buried by a snowdrift. The white fur wasn't the hide of some animal, it sprouted from the hide of a creature that had once been human.

They do exist. The furry fucking Variants are real.

"Fox 1, Ghost 1, do you copy, over?"

Mapes ignored the transmission and crouched to check the body. Master Sergeant Fitzpatrick would have to wait.

Carol held his SAW at the ready while Mapes used a shaking hand to brush off a layer of snow from the cold flesh of a beast he had only heard stories about. The fur was long and tangled from the back to the head like a mane on a lion.

Was this one of the Inuit locals?

Mapes pulled his hand away and used the muzzle of his shotgun to roll the corpse over for a better look. As soon as he poked the flesh, a scream rose over the whistling wind.

Twisting, he watched Johns stumbling in the middle of the street with something sticking out of his stomach.

"Johns!" Carol yelled.

Another scream. This time it was Boston, but Mapes couldn't see the young Marine.

Lance Corporal Johns staggered another foot, turned, and fell to his knees, a spear through his midsection.

Mapes pulled his shotgun away from the corpse and stood, his mind trying to grasp what he was seeing.

Carol was already running back to the street, and Dixon and Preston had stepped out of the other building.

"On me!" Mapes yelled. He moved to join them but something caught his leg. He looked back down at the corpse. This person wasn't dead after all.

Time slowed as his view shifted to a woman with wild white fur stared up at him with two different colored eyes. The left was the yellow slotted iris of a Variant, but the other was brown like his own. Her lips curled into a snarl. They were not the bulging sucker lips of a monster, but jagged, yellow teeth that clanked together from her bloodied gums.

She was some sort of Variant, but human at the same time—a hybrid.

He snapped alert as she swiped at him with a knife. The blade slashed through his left calf before he could move. He stumbled back a few feet and swung his shotgun around, but her knife was already on its way. This time he moved quickly enough to avoid the blade, and it sailed over his shoulder.

A screech. Then a choking sound.

Mapes didn't have a chance to turn to see what the hell was making it.

"You piece of—" He took aim but the woman dashed behind the wall of the shack.

Jesus, she's fast.

Mapes gritted his teeth from the pain racing up his leg, and the anger from the ambush. Adrenaline emptied into his system, prompting a wave of energy.

When he turned to find a target, Carol was on the ground gripping his neck. Blood oozed from between his gloved fingers. The knife the hybrid woman had thrown had hit him right in the jugular.

Mapes knew there wasn't anything he could do for Carol. Johns was dying too, his body jerking in the snow in the center of the street.

Boston was gone.

Dixon and Preston were chasing something to the north toward the foothills.

"Get back here!" Mapes yelled.

They vanished over a hill.

Cursing, Mapes checked for targets again, and then

took a knee next to Carol. The corporal was choking on his own blood. The awful gurgling sound made Mapes cringe.

"It's okay, man. You're going to be okay," he lied. It wasn't the first time he had said that to a dying brother.

Carol's eyes widened behind his goggles and flitted from Mapes to the sky.

In a swift motion, Mapes twisted with his shotgun and blasted a figure that was leaping off the roof of the shack.

A body slammed into the snow to Carol's right, face down, arms and legs spread wide, and a gaping hole in the middle of their back.

Mapes stood and swept his gun from left to right and then back again. There was no sign of Boston, and Johns was as still as a board now. Preston and Dixon were gone.

By the time Mapes looked back down at Carol, the man was dead. His hands fell limply from his neck, revealing the blade that had torn through his flesh.

Mapes scanned for hostiles in the storm. Snow fluttered from the sky, caking his visor with flakes. He wiped them away and then reached down to close Carol's eyes. No one deserved to die in this icy hell. Cold and alone.

"I'm sorry, brother," he whispered.

Down two men, and separated from the other two, Sergeant Jackson Mapes limped away. For the second time in as many days, he had lost half his team.

"It had to have been a Reaver," Dohi said. "That's why I

can't find tracks. It must have swooped down and grabbed Stevenson when we were inside searching."

Team Ghost had sought shelter from the storm under the awning of a house on the edge of town. The village was empty. Completely empty. Not a single body, nor any evidence of what happened to these people. No blood. No tracks. Not even a skeleton. The entire village gave him the creeps and with Stevenson missing, Fitz was losing his cool.

"Did you hear that?" Rico asked.

"What?" Fitz asked. He stepped out into the flurry of snow and looked northwest. Over the growl of the wind came the unmistakable boom of a shotgun.

"Gunfire," Rico said.

Fitz glared at the frosted foothills. Waves of snow poured from the sky. Visibility was getting worse, but his ears told him what his eyes could not.

Fox Team was in trouble.

The shotgun blast had come from that direction. He stepped back to the protection of the building, pulled his bandana down, and pushed the mic back to his lips while Tanaka, Rico, and Dohi stared at him.

"Mapes," Fitz snapped. "Mapes, do you fucking copy?"

For the second time there was no response.

Fitz cursed again.

All it takes is all you got, Marine. Fitz repeated the motto three times before he started to feel better.

"Is that Fox Team?" Tanaka said. "It's got to be, right?"

"What are you orders, Fitz?" Rico asked.

Her firm and formal question got Fitz's attention. They had seen a lot in the past week, but there was nothing like losing a teammate. He knew he had to make a decision, and make one quick. But first, he needed to get a read on Dohi.

The man was crouched and calm in the snow, staring at the storm with his M4 cradled across his chest.

"You can't find a single trace of Stevenson?"

Dohi shook his head. "He's gone."

"But why didn't we hear a gunshot, or a scream? And where the hell is everyone else?" Rico asked. She chomped on her gum, her big eyes widening.

Apollo's tail was still up, but for the first time, Fitz didn't trust the dog's senses. Maybe it was the cold, or perhaps it was something else, but Apollo hadn't been able to detect a single Variant.

Fitz pulled his bandana back up. "We have to keep moving. Stevenson is gone. We have to accept that and focus on the mission—"

"Ghost 1, Ghost 1…." Crackle. "Fox 1, do you…"

Fitz reached up to cup his hand over his helmet.

"Roger, Fox 1... Mapes, what the hell is going on out there?"

"They got my team." Static broke the next transmission.

Rico caught Fitz's gaze.

"Come again, Fox 1."

"Carol and Johns are dead. Boston's gone. Fuck. I can't find Preston or Dixon."

"Calm down," Fitz said. "Calm down and tell me what happened."

There was another flurry of static, and then, "The locals, man. I think it's the locals that took 'em."

Dohi stood, narrowed brows painted white with snow.

"Where are you, Mapes?" Fitz asked. "Tell me where you are, and *stay put*."

"I'm heading for the rally point."

Fitz shook his head. "Mapes, listen to me. You need to hunker down and wait for us. You're not going to make it to the rally point."

Another flurry of static broke over the line.

Fitz nearly ripped his earpiece from his ear. He took in a breath, exhaled, and focused. Team Ghost was down a man, and now, apparently both of the other fire-teams were KIA.

Tanaka, Rico, Dohi, and Apollo waited for orders as the wind swirled snow around the shack. Fitz hated leaving the village without Stevenson, but they had no choice.

Flashing a hand motion, Fitz ordered Team Ghost toward the foothills. It was the first time he had left a man behind since taking command, and he had a feeling it wouldn't be the last. The burden ate at his marrow, but like Captain Reed Beckham had taught him, Fitz pushed on for the sake of his entire team.

4

Preston and Dixon were gone, and Mapes hadn't found a single piece of them. He blinked away the stars before his vision and stopped to look at his leg. Blood oozed from the makeshift tourniquet and dotted the snow. He was leaving a trail of red, but for some reason the beasts that had picked off Fox Team back in the village hadn't attacked him.

He raised his gun and continued his trek north toward the foothills. His boots sank ankle-deep into the snow drifts. The fresh powder was coming down fierce, stinging his exposed face, and working through his layers. He could hardly make out the outline of the trees in the surrounding forest. Skeletal branches groaned under the weight of the snow.

The deeper he ventured into the woods the harder it was to see. A crack, and then a snap like the pop of joints sounded to his right. He whirled with his shotgun toward the sound just as a branch snapped and crashed to the ground. Another crack came from his left, and he swung his gun toward another canopy strained by the weight of the snow.

"Preston, Dixon, do you copy?" he muttered into his headset, although he knew it wouldn't do any good.

Static and the whistle of the wind was the only reply.

His team was gone.

Wiped out in minutes.

Mapes couldn't believe his fucking luck. He had survived the apocalypse back home only to have Europe and now Greenland, shit on him.

He took another step, his boots sinking. The pain in his leg was getting worse, and the cold was numbing his senses.

Another step.

A voice came over the comm line and froze him mid-step.

"Sergeant Mapes… Do you… Help!"

Over the wind, Mapes thought he heard a scream that sounded like Preston. The voice seemed to blend with the wind making the storm sound alive.

"Preston, goddammit, report your location," Mapes said into his mic. "Where the hell are you?"

This time only the screech of wind replied.

His heart caught in his throat when he saw a cloak of white dart between the bases of two trees. Mapes raised his gun and moved his finger from the outside to the inside of the trigger guard.

"Come on, you bastards… show yourselves…"

He jerked the muzzle to the west, then the east. Over the wind came a guttural, animalistic panting and the creaking of joints. There were at least two of them out there, hunting him. Whatever these things were—hybrid, monster, or human—they didn't care if he heard them.

They were taunting him.

He tracked another flash of white to the east and pulled the trigger. The shotgun blast spread out and punched into the base of a tree behind the camouflaged creature. The shot echoed through the forest, and when it was gone, the sounds of the beasts had faded as well. He knew they were still out there, but he'd bought himself some time.

He limped ahead, the blood loss starting to make him light headed.

Stay with it you old bastard. You are not dying on this turd of ice.

He blinked again and again until his vision cleared enough to make out the fort of trees lining the bottom of the foothills. He was almost to the target.

Mapes waited a few minutes to make sure he was alone and then walked to the safety of a massive tree. Another gust of wind slammed through the woods. Limbs caked with snow swung and creaked above him.

He raked his gun over the terrain just to make sure it wasn't one of the creatures sneaking up with him. After a second pass, he crouched uncomfortably and pulled his map and compass.

The village was a half-mile behind him now and he was a quarter mile to the base of the facility. He double-checked his math, and then tucked both items back in his vest.

"Preston, Dixon, do you copy?" The wasted words trailed off to static. He checked his leg again and then reloaded his shotgun.

Almost there... Just keep moving.

A chill shot up his back as he stood. In his peripheral, a figure to the north. Something was watching him. He slowly turned and raised his gun at a naked man standing between two trees. Shoulder-length black hair hung over his face; gray fur slid over his shoulders, and blue veins webbed across exposed skin the color of snow.

The man rolled his head back and flexed lean muscles across his furry frame as he let out a guttural roar. Mapes centered his shotgun on the man's chest, but before he could pull the trigger, dozens of figures leapt from piles of snow in the forest. Male, female, some clothed, some naked, all came running.

The sight of so many creatures sucked the freezing air from Mapes's lungs. He fired off a blast that hit the black-haired man in the chest. Fresh blood coated the white like a bucket of paint had been kicked over.

Mapes snapped into survival mode. Firing to his left then his right, he back peddled through the powder. Spent shells ejected as he fired. The hybrid beasts were fast. Several dropped to all fours and galloped toward him while others leapt to the trees. More came from the direction of the Nazi facility that Mapes was starting to think he was never going to see.

"Fox 1... Can you hear me? This is Ghost 1. Do you copy?"

"I'm under attack!" Mapes yelled back.

"Where?" Fitz replied. "Where the fuck are you?"

"In the forest! Not far from the target!"

Mapes ignored the next transmission, squeezing off

another shot that took the top off the head of a thick male with a mane of black hair. The monster dropped to his knees, brain sloshing out his broken head.

"Fox 1, what the hell is going on out there?"

Mapes didn't have time to reply. He continued firing, hitting a female in the stomach. Her guts splattered on the snow. Mapes wondered if part of Fox Team was inside the steaming pile.

The boom of his shotgun echoed through the forest with screech of the monsters. They fanned out in all directions, making it nearly impossible to kill them. He counted fourteen, but more seemed to be emerging from the sheets of snow in the distance.

"Come on!" Mapes yelled. He jerked the gun up to fire on a smaller beast that had climbed a tree behind him. The blast hit the creature in the side, blowing out a hunk of flesh and exposing the ribcage.

Mapes whirled to shoot a female on all fours skittering over the powder with a knife gripped beneath her yellow teeth.

What the hell were these things?

He centered his muzzle on the beast as she leapt to two feet, knife now in hand.

Click. Click.

Mapes cursed, dropped the shotgun, and went to pull his M9 as the creature tossed the blade at him. He flinched to the left at the last second. The knife was meant for his neck, but sheared off a piece of his trap muscle instead. Warm blood trickled through his layers.

The beast squawked in anger and Mapes screamed in

pain. It dropped back to all fours and barreled toward him. He pulled his M9 from the cold holster and fired three shots that punched through her throat, chest, and stomach. He side-stepped out of the way and she somersaulted and came to a rest in the snow. Blood gushed from the wounds as she bled out next to him.

She sucked in frozen breaths and stared up at him, one of her hands twitching as if she was trying to raise it. He walked past her, saving his bullets for the dozen other creatures prowling and forming a circle around him. Several of them stood on all fours and peaked out from behind the safety of the trees to growl at him.

These were not adult Variants, and they weren't human. He had never seen any of the monsters carry weapons. Why would they need them? They were weapons in themselves, and yet two of the females he had killed carried knives.

Mapes raked his M9 from target to target but held his fire. They shied from the gun now like they understood it could kill them. Variants didn't usually do that. These things had more reasoning, like the Juveniles.

He plucked a grenade from his vest in case they decided to rush him. Blowing himself up sounded better than getting torn to shreds.

The grenade seemed to scare the monsters even more. Several of them darted into the curtain of snow and back into the forest, vanishing into the mist of white.

"You want some?" he said, pointing the gun and grenade at a half naked male that remained. It snarled back then ducked behind a tree.

"How about you?" He directed the weapons at a smaller

creature with a carpet of hair sprouting from its back. It was crouched in a cat-like hunch, waiting to strike. As soon as he moved his trigger finger from the M9 to the pin on the grenade it backed away.

One by one, the beasts slowly retreated back into the storm.

Mapes kept his finger wrapped around the pin and scanned the terrain, struggling to catch his breath. Blood leaked down his chest, but he didn't dare take his eyes off the forest.

He had found the missing villagers, and if he was going to die he was going to bring them with him. If he pulled the pin it would blow him to pieces and detonate the C4 in his rucksack. There was enough in there to blow up half the forest.

"Yeah, that's fucking right. Run. Run or take you all with me!"

He glimpsed a flash of motion that came so fast he couldn't react. His yell was followed by a guttural *oompf!* A tree branch hit him in the dead center of his chest with such force it lifted him into the air. He was thrown backward several feet; his arms and legs spread-eagled as he sailed through the air and hit something that felt like a wall. The most intense pain he had ever experienced shot through his entire body. Stars broke before his eyes, and then, darkness.

Mapes blinked, struggling to stay conscious. Through tunnel vision, a new figure lumbered through the gusting wind on two feet. Unlike the other beasts, this one was far larger with barreled chest muscles and bulging biceps. Its flesh was covered in tangled, gray fur. Instead of clothes, it wore ridged armor plates on its arms, legs, and chest. Now Mapes knew what had killed the juvenile back in the shed at the church near their LZ.

"What the fuck," Mapes choked. He could hardly speak. Hell, he couldn't even move. It took every inch of energy to even crane his head.

The creature strode forward, stopping when it was ten feet away to tilt a head that looked oddly human aside from the overgrown fur on its face. Something hung from its beard...

Mapes squinted at the dried body parts; a shriveled eye tied to the hair, an ear, and...

The creature's yellow-slotted eye on the left and blue eye on the right focused on Mapes. He squirmed and tried to raise his M9, but he couldn't move anything below his neck. He dropped his head and saw the gun was gone. That's when he realized the tree limb that had hit him was not a limb at all.

The long handle of a spear protruded from his chest. The blade had pinned him and his rucksack full of C4 to the tree like a thumbtack pinning a butterfly to a wall. If he had to guess, the tip had sheared his spine below his ribcage.

Mapes choked on blood and coughed. The pain was gone now, replaced by something he hadn't felt in a long time.

Fear was an odd thing. It could be more paralyzing than any other emotion. But Mapes wasn't afraid of dying. He was afraid of being left out here in this godforsaken ice jungle.

The beast crouched to study him, sniffing the air. Its bi-colored eyes flitted from him to the ground near his boots. He followed its gaze to the grenade in the snow.

In a swift motion, the beast turned and darted away, leaving Mapes to die, alone, and paralyzed in the frozen forest.

Fitz led Team Ghost toward a fence of trees. The shotgun blasts had come from somewhere inside over thirty minutes ago. He stopped to listen, but heard nothing over the screaming wind.

Sheets of thick snowflakes fell from the sky, air-brushing everything with white. The soft powder stuck to Fitz's carbon fiber blades. A hundred things were running through his mind and none of them were good. But there was a mission to complete and he still held onto a seed of hope that Stevenson was alive.

If he was, he was somewhere through the forest ahead. Fitz had a feeling they would find Stevenson eventually, perhaps in the lab facility.

Fitz directed Dohi to take point and then gestured for Apollo to go with him. Together, the two trackers set off into the forest. Fitz led Rico and Tanaka after them.

The tips of the trees rose toward the sky of white, branches swaying and shifting. Cracks and groans came from all directions like they were on a wood boat in violent seas.

They were moving quickly, as one, keeping close instead of combat intervals. Whatever was out here was cunning enough to fool both Dohi and Apollo, and they had already slaughtered Fox Team. Judging by the lack of gunshots, Mapes was dead now too.

Fitz focused on Dohi's outline through the snow. Apollo trotted alongside, sniffing, wagging his tail, then sniffing some more. For a moment, the sight reminded Fitz of Beckham. Fitz loved the dog, and the Shepherd loved him, but Apollo was Beckham's dog, and Fitz felt guilty for bringing him all this way.

Just make sure you bring him home in one piece, Beckham had said.

Fitz exhaled and whispered, "I'll bring him home, brother. Soon."

The thought of seeing his friends again gave Fitz the boost of energy he needed. He walked a bit faster, knowing they were closing in on the target. Get in, find the weapon, blow the place up, and get out. That was all they had to do now. Well that, and survive. And find Stevenson.

Fitz worked his fingers in his gloves to keep the blood flowing. He needed to be ready to fire at a second's notice, and the cold had already penetrated every layer. He raised his M4 when Dohi froze ahead. The tracker balled his hand and crouched next to Apollo. The dog trotted a few feet forward, his muzzle going to work before stopping at a mound that looked like a red snow cone.

Flashing a hand signal, Fitz ordered his team to toward the gore. As he approached he prepared himself to find a body, but instead, there was only a flattened area covered in fresh blood.

Dohi plucked something out of the snow and held it up. He tossed away a shotgun shell and looked up when Fitz arrived.

"Looks like a battlefield," Dohi whispered. He stood and

jerked his chin toward the north where bloodstains littered the snow.

Fitz wiped the snow from his goggles.

"But where are all the bodies?" Rico asked.

"On me," Fitz said. He led the team through the site of a battle, searching for evidence of whatever had happened. Every few feet he spotted a shotgun shell and blood, but there was no sign of a corpse.

Fitz stopped mid-stride when he felt eyes on him. Dohi had already stopped.

"What?" Rico whispered. "Why are we stopped?"

Another voice came in the respite of the whistling wind. It was faint, and sounded strangled. Fitz followed Dohi's gaze to the northeast. Through the gusting snow, he saw a figure against a tree.

Fitz flashed a set of motions for Ghost to spread out. With their weapons shouldered, they slowly approached the contact.

Squinting to see the man's face, Fitz hoped to God it wasn't Stevenson, The man's head was slumped against his chest, and a wood pole had him pinned to the tree. Blood blossomed around his white uniform and vest, leaking down his stomach and legs. As Fitz approached he saw exposed, pale skin.

It was one of Fox Team, but there was no way the man could still be alive.

Fitz directed Rico and Tanaka to watch their six and then approached the tree with Dohi and Apollo. They stopped a few feet away, and Fitz reached out to lift the man's head to see Sergeant Mapes. His lips were blue, and ice hung from his nose.

"Damn," Fitz whispered. He slowly pulled his fingers

from Mapes's chin to set his head back on his chest and looked to Dohi.

"Help..."

Fitz's heart leapt and he redirected his gaze toward Mapes.

"He's alive," Dohi whispered.

Purple, lips trembling, Mapes tried to talk.

"Water," he mumbled. "Need. Water."

Dohi pulled his water bottle, and Mapes craned his neck, wincing in pain, and tonguing the water

"Hypothermia. Makes the body hot," Dohi whispered. "We got to get him down from the tree."

Fitz nodded, but Mapes shook his head and coughed.

"No," he said. "I can't move anything below my neck. Do me a solid, Master Sergeant. Put one in my head."

Dohi and Fitz exchanged a look.

Fitz had killed out of mercy before, but shooting out here would tell whatever was out there where they were. They would have to knife him instead, but Fitz wasn't sure he could do that.

"Tell us what you saw. Tell us what did this," Dohi said.

Mapes swallowed. "Some sort of..." He coughed and his eyes rolled up into his head.

Fitz grabbed Mapes's cheeks in his gloves and said, "Tell us what you saw, Mapes. We have to know."

Redirecting his eyes, Mapes focused on Fitz.

A branch snapped in the distance, and a pile of snow fell to the ground.

Mapes choked again. "I saw demons. Not Variant. Not human. Something in between."

Fitz glanced down at the spear shaft protruding from Mapes's chest. Whatever had thrown it had done so with such force that it had torn through flesh, bone, and a rucksack. He slowly let go of Mapes's face and took a step back.

"After you complete your mission, come back for my body. Don't leave me out here," Mapes mumbled. "Promise me, Fitz."

Fitz turned toward another snapping tree branch that brought a mound of snow down. When he looked back at Mapes, the man was gone. His head slumped against his chest.

"I promise, brother."

5

The lab entrance was easier to find than Fitz had thought. All he had to do was find the poles with Variant and human corpses flung up on display outside a bluff covered in snow and trees.

He pulled his bandana and scarf up over his nose to keep out the stench. It didn't matter that these bodies were frozen; they still reeked of rot and sour fruit.

The sheets of snow had lessened, providing a view of the entire graveyard. There were dozens of the monsters hanging from crucifixes, plus the soldiers from the tape recording Team Ghost had listened to on the flight in. The human bodies were torn apart, their faces unrecognizable from deep gashes and swollen flesh, now frozen. Behind the bodies was the tunnel leading into the hills.

"It's a warning," Dohi said. "My grandfather told me stories about something like this when I was a boy."

Fitz remembered a book in high school about medieval armies posting their enemies on pikes. Dohi was right, this was a warning, but it was also a psychological game designed to scare the enemy.

Team Ghost would not be deterred.

The mission would continue, but at what cost?

Fitz was down a man, and the other two fire teams were wiped out. At least he knew what monsters were out there. According to Mapes, the creatures that had done this were the locals—some sort of hybrid beast. From what Fitz had seen, they could use weapons and set traps. Not the type of traps or ambushes Alpha Variants or Juveniles were known for. These things were experts at hiding. Even Dohi couldn't find them. And apparently they saw any outsider as a threat—human or monster.

"Fitz," Rico said. "What should—"

"Watch for bobby traps and keep your eyes on those trees," Fitz said. "We're proceeding with the mission."

Rico hesitated, but didn't protest. She continued with the rest of the team. They spread out through the maze of corpses. Fitz knew each and every member of Ghost was on edge, but they were prepared for this, and he was proud to have them by his side. Most men and women wouldn't dare follow him and Ghost into the fray.

He walked up to the corpse of a Juvenile hanging on a cross a few feet away. Every single plate of armor was gone, leaving exposed flesh and stringy muscle.

Fitz continued on with his gun shouldered. A bird

pecked at the face of a human soldier near the entrance to the lab facility. It continued stripping away ribbons of flesh with its black beady eyes on Team Ghost.

Above the bird, the concrete lip of the tunnel had been etched into a bluff topped with a forest. Fitz couldn't read the sign, but he had a feeling it said, *No Trespassing*. An iron-rod gate was left ajar in front of the tunnel and a pickup truck covered in snow was parked outside.

Fitz continued through the macabre display of corpses, sweeping the area with his M4. A mini-forest covered much of the foothills in this area, leaving multiple blind zones. His first scan revealed nothing but branches and frosted trees, but he could feel something watching him—something was out there, waiting to strike.

Dohi and Apollo stopped when they got to the pickup. Rico and Tanaka took up position behind the vehicle and Fitz approached the door. He glanced down at Apollo, his heart leaping when he saw the dog's tail. It was down. For the first time today, Apollo could sense the monsters.

"Something's watching us," Dohi said. "In the woods."

Fitz raised his rifle toward the tree line. He swept the crosshairs across the base of trees and the branches, but nothing moved in the winter wasteland.

Lowering his rifle, Fitz considered past missions. Back then he was just a Marine following Beckham. Now he was in Beckham's role. What would Captain Beckham do? He had to have known when he infiltrated Building 8 seven months ago that there was something inside. But he proceeded anyway. That's what soldiers did.

Every member of Team Ghost looked to Fitz for orders,

and he felt the burn of the heavy burden all leaders carried when they led men and women into battle.

There was only one thing to say. "Stay frosty, and stay sharp."

Fitz jerked his chin around the side of the pickup toward the tunnel entrance, trying his best to manage his heart rate and breathing with positive thoughts.

Dohi was first past the gate. He squeezed through the opening and walked into a long tunnel that stretched deep into the hills.

Fitz and Apollo went next and then Rico and Tanaka. The concrete ceiling was low, maybe ten feet, but the walls were wide enough for vehicles to pass through. Snow covered the ground through most of the tunnel. Fitz searched for tracks, but saw none.

"Dohi, you think there is another entrance to the lab?" Fitz asked.

"I'm sure of it," Dohi said. "My guess is those things have a back door."

Rico stopped and studied the wall to their right. "Where are all the bullet holes?"

Dohi spat on the ground and adjusted his rifle. "I'm sure we'll find some soon."

Fitz nodded. "Keep moving. We should be coming up on the main entrance."

They walked for several minutes, the light and the screeching wind dwindling behind them. It felt good to be out of the cold, but Fitz had a feeling he was trading the freezing temperatures for something much worse.

He turned to check his six and pulled up his goggles just

as a curtain of flesh darted on the other side of the fence. It was gone in a blink of an eye.

"What?" Rico asked. "Why are you stopping?"

"Thought I saw something."

Dohi halted at the corner ahead where the passage narrowed. He balled his hand into a fist and waited.

Fitz glanced back at the gate once more and then motioned his team to continue around the bend. Side by side they approached a blast door that was wide open. Apollo sat on his hind legs a few feet from the steel and stared into a hallway that led inside the facility.

"What do make of this, Master Sergeant?" Dohi asked.

"I was about to ask you the same thing," Fitz said.

Rico dipped her head from side to side. "I really don't like this."

"Why would they just keep the door open?" Tanaka said.

"We're going to find out. Shoot anything that moves like a Variant. " Fitz put a hand out and touched Rico's sleeve. "Stay close to me."

She pulled the gum from her mouth and stuck it to her helmet. "You stay close to me."

Fitz almost grinned. Instead, he flicked the tactical light on his M4 and nodded at Dohi. One by one, beams shot out and angled into the hallway. The tile floor was covered in snowy footprints. There were boot and shoe marks as well, but the majority seemed to be bare feet.

Dohi bent to examine one, then glanced back up at Fitz. "Looks like Variant to me. Nothing human could walk around barefoot out there for long."

"On me," Fitz said. He had a rule: never let someone do

something he could do himself. If they were walking into a trap, he was going to be the first one in.

The team entered the hallway single file, lights dancing across the ceiling and the glass windows framing the sides of the passage. Fitz had no idea what the layout of the lab was, or where the weapon they were looking for might be, but this didn't look like any BSL4 lab he had seen.

They passed windows overlooking offices furnished with leather chairs and metal desks. The walls were white, but there was no lab equipment, and there was no entrance to the offices from the hallway. The odd architecture gave Fitz the chills. *What kind of lab is this?*

"Start setting the C4," he said.

Dohi and Tanaka placed the charges on the outside of the walls and then gathered back behind Fitz.

The hallway ended at another door. He shone his beam at the steel frame and the white bars lining a glass panel window. Approaching slowly, Fitz examined the exterior. The paint had been peeled away, revealing a Swastika. Another chill raced through his body.

He stood, grabbed the handle and jerked his helmet at Rico. She took up position behind him with Apollo next to her. Tanaka and Dohi hung back, watching their rear guard.

Fitz twisted the knob. It clicked. *Unlocked.* He opened the door for Rico. She moved into another hallway, Fitz and Apollo right behind her.

Team Ghost slowly worked the passage with peeling paint and concrete walls. The Nazis had built this place to withstand a bombing run by the Allied Forces that never happened. It had survived all these years, buried and unknown to most of the world.

Fitz made it a quarter way down before he stopped to take a closer look through more glass windows. He directed his light inside the one on his left—a small room furnished with a metal bench, toilet, and sink. Metal bars served as a barrier between the cell and the windows. But where was the entrance?

He flicked his light toward the ceiling where a trap door was sealed shut. *What in the hell?*

Fitz continued to the next window. The next two rooms were the same holding cells with ceiling entrances.

Rico checked the windows across the hall and then looked back at Fitz, her eyes wide. She didn't need to say anything. Fitz could see she was spooked.

They pressed on, nearing the halfway mark of the passage where the first sign of a battle emerged. Bullet holes dotted the ceiling and walls. Carmine stains caked the walls where the soldiers from Greenland and the EUF had perished.

"I thought this was a lab," Rico whispered. "Looks more like an insane asylum."

"Makes you wonder what type of weapon they were working on to kill the Juveniles," Tanaka said. He placed more C4 charges on the walls and the windows.

At the end of the hallway lay another open door. Fitz had a feeling they were about to find the answer to Tanaka's question. He gripped his M4 tighter, and gestured for Apollo to get behind him.

With the wave of his hand, Fitz ordered Team Ghost forward into a large space the size of a gymnasium. At the center of the room was a pit that could have been a very deep swimming pool drained of water. A metal fence with razor wire surrounded the opening. Thirty feet above, a metal platform with a balcony overlooked the room. There were several steel doors on the wall, all sealed shut. It was some sort of observation post, but to observe what?

Fitz strode into the room, sweeping his rifle back and forth. Nothing stirred in the massive place.

"Clear," he said. He motioned for his team to spread out. Apollo suddenly stopped and growled at the fence. Fitz moved his finger from the outside of his trigger guard to the trigger and focused his light on the thick chain-link fence. As he approached, a drop of liquid plummeted in front of his weapon and plopped to the ground in front of his blades.

Fitz slowly tilted his head toward the domed ceiling and angled his light. Three human bodies were suspended by their feet.

"Stevenson," Rico said.

Fitz raked his light over the bodies. His heart hammered in his chest when he saw she was right. Stevenson dangled from the middle of the ceiling like a chandelier, a cord wrapped around his feet. The other two men were from Fox Team. From his vantage, Fitz couldn't tell if they were alive. He put his finger to his lips to keep Rico quiet, but she didn't get the message.

"We have to cut them down."

Fitz cursed under his breath, glared at her, and then flashed hand signals to Dohi and Tanaka. They were already looking for a way up.

Apollo stalked toward the fence surrounding the pit,

continuing his low growl. Fitz approached cautiously and peered through the chain links into a pit thirty feet deep. Metal spikes the size of buck knives lined the walls like barbed cobwebs.

He directed his light toward the bottom. On the floor next to a metal bench rested a bowl and a bucket. He glanced back up at Stevenson and the other two soldiers hanging from the ceiling. Why not keep them in one of the rooms or even the pit if they were prisoners? Why hang them up there?

Nothing made sense, why would… Fitz shook the questions away as Tanaka climbed a ladder to the balcony. Dohi had frozen on the floor beneath the balcony.

"Back!" he shouted just as the doors on the top level swung open. They disgorged furry figures onto the platform; joints popping like the branches back in the frozen woods.

A thud behind him made Fitz's heart leap again. The exit to the room had been slammed shut. He twisted and yelled, "Ghost, on me!"

They came together in the center of the room as the platform filled with the creatures that had killed every soldier that had set foot in this cursed place.

Fitz focused on the silhouette of a thick man that stood in front of Team Ghost's exit door. In his right hand he held a long spear, and in his left he gripped a shield made from a Juvenile torso. More of the rigged armor lined his extremities, chest, and genitals.

"I killed you…" Fitz whispered, a memory of the Bone Collector Alpha rising in his mind. "I blew your fucking head off."

The creature strode into the light of Rico's rifle giving Fitz his first glance at the monster. This beast was not the Bone Collector—this was something far worse. Body parts hung from a tangled beard. It flexed barreled chest muscles and snorted at Fitz as it studied him with a yellow slotted eye and one blue one.

This *wasn't* a lab. This was a prison where the scientists had used some sort of weapon to infect the local Inuits, turning them into monsters that hunted Juveniles and, apparently, humans.

But for some reason they weren't attacking. The dozen creatures on the balcony remained in the shadows, staring down and holding weapons: knives, spears, even a bow and arrow. All of the blades were angled at Team Ghost.

"Hold your fire," Fitz ordered his team.

"What?" Rico muttered. "You crazy?"

"We're surrounded," Fitz said. "There's no fighting out of this one. Maybe we can reason with these things."

"That sounds like a bad idea. Variants, don't reason." Rico stepped in front of Fitz, but he pulled her back. Tanaka and Dohi flanked them as the Alpha lumbered forward, snorting again and scanning Fitz and his men. It pounded its chest and raised the spear, but didn't throw it.

"Finally," the beast said with a snort. His voice was almost human, but the voice box seemed atrophied, like the man had smoked cigars his entire life.

"I've been watching you. Watching you all."

Fitz swallowed hard, and said, "What do you want?"

The beast pointed the spear at Fitz and grinned with yellow, jagged teeth.

"Finally I have a worthy opponent. Even if you are just half a man."

Fitz almost raised his rifle to shoot the beast, but gritted his teeth instead.

"I would highly recommend..." Rico began to say, but Fitz raised his hand to silence her and took a step forward. Apollo barred his teeth, snarling at the creature, but Fitz would not be deterred.

"You win, and you get to leave with your friends," the creature said. "I win, and... we eat you."

Fitz glanced up at the balcony. More of the hybrid monsters had emerged. They weren't just hunters looking for prey. They were cannibals, too.

"Let us fight," Dohi whispered.

"We can take 'em, Fitz," Tanaka added.

"I agree," Rico said.

"No," Fitz said. Team Ghost had enough firepower to get out of here, but not without taking casualties. It would require trusting the beast. If he fought it and won, then they would all get out of here alive. If he didn't accept the challenge, and fought with his team, then several members of Ghost would die. He couldn't let that happen.

"If I go down, you fight," Fitz whispered. He reached out toward Tanaka. "Give me your Katana."

"All due respect, but ..."

"That's an order," Fitz said as he set his rifles on the ground.

Tanaka unsheathed the blade and reluctantly handed it to Fitz.

The beast's grin widened, and it twirled the spear and

took a step backward. It motioned for the creatures on the balcony to lower their weapons, and Fitz nodded at his team to do the same.

Taking another step, Fitz gripped the Katana in both hands. It felt light, but he knew the blade could cut through Juvenile armor. He had seen Tanaka do it back in France.

"Be careful, Fitzie," Rico whispered.

"Good luck, Master Sergeant," Tanaka said.

Dohi let out a grunt and then said, "Kill this bastard."

Fitz took a deep breath, doing his best to suppress his fear. He was used to fighting with his rifle, not a sword, but with the lives of his team on the line, he had no other choice.

All it takes is all you got!

With the blade out in front, Fitz lunged at the beast. The creature parried the attack with its shield, deflecting the sword. Then it swung the spear at Fitz, the shaft smacking him in the shoulder before he could duck. He screamed out in pain, the stiches in his shoulder tearing.

Stumbling backward, Fitz regained his balance and then swung the blade wide. This time the tip sliced the creature in the leg. It roared in pain, and went down on one knee. Fitz raised the blade above his head, bringing it down as hard as he could like a hammer.

The creature lifted the shield and once again deflected the sword. The clank echoed through the room. That got the monsters above excited.

Animalistic panting sounded from the balcony above as Fitz stumbled backward again, his fingers numb from the vibration. The Juvenile torso was strong, but the Katana blade was stronger. It had chipped a groove into the shield.

The beast pushed to its feet and twirled the shaft above its head, blood dripping from the slash in its thigh. In a quick movement it swiped at Fitz, but this time he ducked beneath the spear. He went down on one knee and lunged with his sword again, striking the monster in the armpit.

He yanked the blade out, a guttural scream reverberating through the room. Fitz struck the shaft of the spear, splintering the wood as the beast struck him in the face with the shield.

Pain lanced up his nose and stars broke across his vision. He slashed with his blade to keep the creature back while he blinked away the fuzz. Bringing a hand up to his face, he felt the warm sticky blood pouring from his nose. It was broken, no doubt about that.

Something hard hit him hard in the chest a moment later, and he crashed to the ground, gasping for air. He blinked again and saw the creature toss the shield away. It used its knee to break through the middle of the spear like a toothpick. Holding the two pieces in each hand, it strode toward Fitz.

"Get up, Fitz!" Rico shouted.

"Come on!" Tanaka yelled.

Grunting and shouts sounded from the balcony.

Fitz winced and pushed himself up. He sliced through the air with the sword as soon as he was on both of his blades. The sword hit one of the shafts, sticking into the wood, but the beast used the other to smack Fitz in his helmet. The rattle shook his brain, and he backed up, blinking away another flurry of stars and fuzz.

"I'm going to enjoy this," the creature said. It let out a

bellowing laugh. In that moment everything froze, and although Fitz couldn't see he could hear the creature preparing to strike.

Blind and desperate, Fitz ducked just as the blade whooshed above his head. Then, with all of his strength, he lunged. The blade cracked through armor, and then sunk into flesh.

Warm liquid peppered his arms, and a scream so loud it hurt his ears followed.

Part human, part monster.

Blinking rapidly, Fitz's vision finally cleared. He had impaled the beast right through the heart.

The other creatures and Team Ghost fell into silence.

Nothing stirred in the massive room.

Fitz winced again, the blood rushing in his ears. He stood and pulled the sword from the beast's chest, a crunching sound echoing. The hybrid man dropped to both armored knees, staring at Fitz with one monster eye and one human. A grin still on its face, the creature crashed to the ground. Blood pooled around the body, spreading toward Fitz's blades. He took a step back and glanced up at the monsters on the balcony.

They continued to glare at their fallen leader as if they expected him to get back up. Rico, Tanaka, and Dohi waited with their weapons at the ready.

A tense moment passed that was shattered by the squawk from a frail female. She let out a pained roar at the team.

Had this creature been the mate of the beast Fitz had killed?

Team Ghost gripped their weapons, ready to raise them

and open fire, but Fitz ordered them to stand down as the beasts slowly withdrew through the open doorways, disappearing into the ancient Nazi facility.

"Holy shit, Fitz," Rico said. "Are you okay?" She lowered her gun and ran over to Fitz with Apollo trotting along.

"I… I think so," Fitz said. A wave of dizziness washed over him and he crouched. "Hurry, get Stevenson and those other men down."

Keep your head above your heart, man. Don't…

Fitz closed his eyes and felt the second rush of blood in his ears. His skull pounded like someone was hitting him with a hammer.

He was going to crash. He couldn't get enough air, and his vision was failing.

Something warm brushed his right hand.

Apollo glanced up, his amber eyes stricken with worry.

"Fitzie!" Rico exclaimed as he collapsed. He fell on his stomach; his arms limp at his sides. He tried to talk, tried to move, but he couldn't fight the darkness. The last thing he saw was the listless yellow slitted and blue eye of the monster he had killed staring back at him.

Fitz woke up on a vibrating floor. His brain felt like applesauce sloshing inside his skull. Ringing echoed in his ears, but there was another noise beyond that, some sort of chopping. And voices. He could hear faint voices.

He struggled to move, wiggling his fingers first, and then his hands. The shades of red and orange framing his vision slowly retreated. All at once, the ringing stopped like the final suck of a vacuum and he heard a soft voice.

"Fitz, you're back."

He put his hand on his head, but where his helmet should have been he felt soft padding.

"Where am I?"

The *whoosh-whoosh* of helicopter blades answered his question.

The bright colors vanished, and in their place, he saw a dead face. Everything came crashing back, and he remembered the beast back at the facility.

But this was no monster.

It was Mapes. His eyelids were closed, and the ice on his five o'clock shadow was already melting. Team Ghost had retrieved his body. Fitz had kept his promise to the man after all.

A few feet behind Mapes lay Stevenson. Dohi and Tanaka hovered over him and applied bandages to wounds that Fitz couldn't see. Two other bodies, both covered by white sheets were resting near the open door.

"Hang on, Ghost," said Tito over the comms. "I'm getting you the hell out of this frozen shit hole!"

Fitz struggled to sit, but Rico pushed back on his chest. Apollo wedged up to his side, resting his head on Fitz's vest.

"Stay put, Fitzie. You took a beating back there," Rico said with a smile. Her dimples were the best thing Fitz had seen all day. She blew a bubble, and her grin widened now that she had his attention.

"If you're going to blow it, now's the time!" Tito said.

Dohi stood and walked over to the open Black Hawk door with something in his hand.

Below, branches from hundreds of trees reached up toward the chopper like skeletal fingers. The tunnel to the Nazi facility and the pickup truck came into focus.

Dohi looked back at Fitz for orders. With a nod, Fitz gave him the all clear.

Raising the detonator, Dohi pushed it once, then twice, and then a third time. Three concussions thudded in the distance, deep and loud. Fireballs shot out of the tunnel entrance, slamming into the gate and flipping the pickup truck. The flames raced over the snow, plowing into the graveyard of human and Juvenile corpses, and slamming through the forest.

The bluff over the facility sagged, cracked, and caved in, sealing the prison where the military had once again tried to play God. The weapon had ended up not being a vile or tube after all. Like VX-99, the weapon designed here had turned the poor souls that had once lived in the fishing village into monsters.

Fitz watched the rooftops pass below, saying a mental prayer for the innocent civilians that had lost their lives. Some of the hybrid creatures might have escaped the inferno and retreated into the forest, and Fitz secretly hoped they might be able to find some sort of peace.

All that mattered now was that Team Ghost had completed their mission. They had killed the monster and destroyed the old Nazi facility. Somehow, once again, Fitz hadn't lost a man, woman, or dog.

But this time he had come very close. Stevenson wasn't

out of the woods yet, either. Fitz crawled over to him and grabbed his hand as Tito flew over the harbor and ocean, returning to the USS Forrest Sherman for fresh orders.

Webb, the Crew Chief, sat across the troop hold, incredulous eyes on Fitz.

"What the hell happened out there, Master Sergeant?" he asked.

Team Ghost had one hell of a story, but Fitz wasn't prepared to tell it now. Instead, he tightened his grip on Stevenson's hand. The man cracked his eyelids and focused on Fitz, his lips trembling.

"Hang in there brother," Fitz whispered. "This battle is over, but we're going back to war."

Ready for Extinction Cycle book 7, War? Join Team Ghost and prepare for all out war by signing up for the spam-free newsletter.: *http://eepurl.com/bggNg9*

Don't forget to check out Trackers, the newest Post-Apocalyptic thriller from Nicholas Sansbury Smith. Download your copy here: *http://amzn.to/2lfZEYh*

Join Nicholas on social media:
Facebook: Nicholas Sansbury Smith
Twitter: https://twitter.com/greatwaveink
Website: www.nicholassansbury.com

ABOUT THE AUTHOR

Nicholas Sansbury Smith is the USA Today bestselling author of the Hell Divers trilogy, the Orbs trilogy, and the Extinction Cycle series. He worked for Iowa Homeland Security and Emergency Management in disaster mitigation before switching careers to focus on his one true passion—writing. When he isn't writing or daydreaming about the apocalypse, he enjoys running, biking, spending time with his family, and traveling the world. He is an Ironman triathlete and lives in Iowa with his fiancée, their dogs, and a house full of books.

CPSIA information can be obtained
at www.ICGtesting.com
Printed in the USA
BVHW040212200820
586886BV00018B/462